김영무-**가상현실**

# Virtual Reality

Poems by **Kim Young-Moo**

Translated by Brother Anthony of Taizé and Jongsook Lee

KB141652

한국문학영역총서

# Virtual Reality

Translated by Brother Anthony of Taizé and Jongsook Lee

Original Poems ⓒ Kim Young-Moo
Translation ⓒ 2005, Brother Anthony, Jongsook Lee

Published by Dap Gae Books
#201 Won Bld. 829-22 Bangbae 4-dong, Seocho-gu, Seoul 137-834 Korea
Tel / (02)591-8267, 537-0464, 596-0464 Fax / 594-0464

The poems "Perth : riverside with swans" and "One morning in Perth" were first published in *Westerly* Volume 49 (2004), a literary magazine published in the University of Western Australia, Perth.

English Translations of Korean Literature Series
Publisher : Jang, So-Nim

김영무-**가상현실**
# Virtual Reality

Poems by **Kim Young-Moo**

Translated by Brother Anthony of Taizé and Jongsook Lee

도선출판 **답게**

# 역자서문

안토니 수사(씀)

(이종숙 역)

2001년 11월 30일, 금요일, 서울 프레스센터 국제회의장은 만해 문학상, 백석 문학상 등 창작과비평사 주관 문학상 시상식에 참석하기 위해 모여든 문인들로 붐볐다. 예년보다 내객도 많고 분위기도 다르게 느껴진 것은 백석 문학상 수상자 김영무가 며칠 전 세상을 떠난 탓이었을까. 그 날 그 곳에 모인 김영무의 친구와 동료에게는 무거운 영결 미사를 치른 지 이틀 만에 찾아온 이 행사가 고인의 삶을 축제로 추억할 수 있는 소중한 기회가 되었다.

김영무는 1944년 경기도 파주에서 태어나 서울대학교 영어영문학과에서 학사와 석사 학위를 받은 후, 미국 뉴욕 주립대학 스토니 브룩 캠퍼스에서 조지 엘리옷에 대한 논문으로 영문학 박사 학위를 받았으며, 1982년 모교 영문학과에 교수로 취임하여 2001년 11월 26일 세상을 떠날 때까지 재직했다.

1975년 김영무는 「이육사론」을 발표하면서 등단하여 문학 비평 활동을 펼치는 한편, 윌리엄 블레이크의 시를 비롯한 종교적

주제를 다룬 영문학 작품을 다수 번역했을 뿐 아니라 틈틈이 수필을 발표하였다. 1990년에는 문학 비평서 『시의 언어와 삶의 언어』를 발표하여 이듬해 1991년에 한국 문학상을 수상했다. 김영무는 또한 독실한 천주교 신자이기도 하였다.

김영무는 1991년부터 2년 간 토론토 대학 방문 교수로 캐나다에 거주하면서 현지의 우리 말 신문에 시를 기고하기 시작하여, 1992년에는 캐나다 거주 한국인 5명과 함께 토론토에서 시집을 출판했다. 1993년 귀국 후부터는 국내의 여러 문예 잡지에 시를 기고하다가 같은 해 5월 첫 시집을 내놓았고, 폐암으로 수술받은 후, 병원에서 투병중이던 1998년 8월 두 번째 시집을 발표하였다. 가능한 모든 의술을 동원하더라도 몇 달밖에 여명이 없다는 진단을 받은 김영무는 자신의 몸에 훼손을 가하는 어떤 치료법도 거부하고, 자석 요법, 자연식 요법, 걷기 요법과 같은 섭생법을 택했다. 의사들의 예상보다 훨씬 더 오래 생존한 김영무는 1999년부터 1년 간 오스트레일리아 퍼스에서 가족과 함께 머무르며 요양하면서 시작詩作에 열중했다. 그는 그 때 쓴 울루루 연작시와 투병의 고통이 가르쳐 준 삶과 죽음의 노래를 한데 담아 2001년 4월 마지막 시집 『가상현실』을 발표했다. 그 때 이미 병석에서 일어날 수 없는 몸이 되어 버린 김영무는 이 시집으로 제3회 백석 문학상 수상자가 되었다. 그러나 그 상은 며칠 일찍 눈을 감은 그를 대신하여 그의 아내가 받아야했다.

세상을 떠나기 전 마지막 며칠 동안에 준비한 백석 문학상 수상 소감문에서 김영무는 시가 자신을 찾아온 순간을 이렇게 묘

사한다. 토론토 근처 어떤 수도원 교회에서 십자가 하나를 보았는데 특이하게도 거기에는 예수의 몸이 아니라 피조물 초록빛 지구가 면류관을 쓰고 피를 흘리며 매달려 있더라는 것이다. 그 형상을 처음 본 순간, 신의 현현을 본 것처럼 마음 속 깊은 곳으로부터 시가 솟아나는 걸 느꼈는데, 그건 아마 수난의 초록 지구 형상이 자신이 평소 가지고 있던 환경에 대한 관심과 천주교의 신앙을 절묘하게 결합한 이미지였기 때문이 아닌가 생각한다는 것이다. 그렇게 보면 김영무의 시가 대부분 캐나다와 오스트레일리아의 거대한 자연에 뿌리박고 그로부터 길어 올린 영감에 의해 쓰인 것도 결코 우연이 아닌 것 같다.

2001년부터 김영무는 온몸으로 퍼진 암세포 때문에 거동할 수 없게 되었지만, 가족의 극진한 보살핌에 힘입어 집에서 글도 쓰고 번역도 하고 친구들도 만나면서 지낼 수 있었다. 이 마지막 투병 기간 중에 김영무는 자신의 시 가운데서 번역하고 싶은 작품을 몇 편 골라 뽑았는데, 여기 이 시집은 바로 그 작품들을 영어로 번역한 것이다.

통증이 견딜 수 없는 정도로 심해진 2001년 11월 20일 김영무는 마침내 병원으로 옮겨져 일주일을 채 못 견디고 11월 26일 오후 7시 30분, 이 세상을 뒤로 하고 떠났다. 죽기 사흘 전 그는 마지막으로 시 한 편을 종이에 옮겼다. 김영무를 알고 사랑했던 우리들은 그 시에서 그가 우리에게 남긴 가장 아름다운 유품을 발견한다.

무지개

이 땅에 시인 하나
풀꽃으로 피어나
바람결에 놀다갔다.

풀무치 새 울음소리 좋아하고
이웃 피붙이 같은 버들치
힘찬 지느러미 짓
더욱 좋아했다.

찬 이슬 색동보석 맺히는
풀섶 세상
― 참 다정도 하다.

2001. 11. 23 평촌에서

# Translator's Introduction

On Friday, November 30, 2001, many literary figures gathered high up in the Seoul Press Center for the annual ceremony at which the Manhae Prize for Literature, the Paeksŏk Prize and other literary awards are made, under the auspices of the literary journal *Changjak gwa bipyŏng* That year the room was more crowded than usual, and the atmosphere was perhaps slightly different because everyone knew that the recipient of the Paeksŏk Prize, Kim Young-Moo, had died only a few days before. Many of his friends and colleagues were glad to have this more festive occasion to remember him after the gravity of his funeral Mass two days previously.

Kim Young-moo was born in 1944 in Paju, near Seoul. After earning his B.A. and M.A. from the English Department of Seoul National University, he received his Ph.D. from the English Department of SUNY at Stony Brook with a dissertation on George Eliot. He became a Professor in the Department of English Language and Literature at Seoul National University in 1982. He died on November 26, 2001.

His first article on Korean poetry, dedicated to the poet Yi

Yuksa, published in 1975, signified his recognition as a literary critic. He published a number of translations from English, including a volume of translations of poems by William Blake, and several works on religious themes. He was a devout Catholic. He published a volume of personal essays in 1988 and a volume of literary criticism on 'The Language of Poetry and the Language of Life' in 1990, which received the prize for criticism in the 1991 Republic of Korea Literary Awards.

In 1991, during a 2-year stay as visiting professor in Toronto (Canada), he began to publish poems in a local Koreanlanguage newspaper. In 1992, he and five others published in Toronto a collection of their poems. He published a number of poems in a journal in Korea early in 1993 and his first volume was published in Seoul in May 1993. A second volume was published while he was still in hospital recovering from an operation for lung cancer in August 1998. Learning that he could not expect to live much longer no matter what the doctors did, he decided not to submit to any treatment that would do further violence to his body. Instead, he adopted a gentle regime involving treatment by magnets, a natural diet, and therapeutic walking.

Surviving far beyond the anticipated few months, he took his family to spend a year together in Perth, Australia in 1999-2000. The poems he composed there include a series of poems about the great sacred rock Uluru, that he was able to visit. His third volume, that included poems inspired by his experience of sickness and those composed in Australia, was published in April 2001, when he was already bedridden. It earned him the 3rd Paeksŏk Literary Award, which his widow received in his place, a few days after his death, on November 30.

In the acceptance speech he had prepared for the Paeksŏk Award ceremony in the last days of his life, he described how he had begun to find poems arising in him after seeing, in the church of a monastery outside Toronto, a crucifix on which was hung an image, not of the human body of Jesus but of the green globe of the natural creation, crowned with thorns and bleeding. This image, combining his own ecological concerns and his Catholic faith, deeply impressed him and the sight of it served as a moment of epiphany. It is surely no coincidence that so much of his poetry was rooted in and inspired by the great natural wildernesses of Canada and Australia.

From early in 2001, he was bedridden by the spreading cancer. Thanks to his family's devoted care, he was able to remain at home, writing, translating, and meeting friends. It was during this period that he made the selection of his poems that he wished to see translated, now published in this volume.

At last the pain became intolerable. He was taken to hospital on November 20 and died at 7:30pm on November

26, 2001. Three days before he died, he wrote a final poem. We who knew and loved him are agreed that in this poem he gave us the very best possible memorial.


Rainbow

In this land one poet
blossomed — a wild flower,
played in the wind, then went away.

He enjoyed the songs of crickets and birds,
enjoyed even more
the sturdy fin-strokes
of minnows, neighborly, kin-like.

The world of wild greenery
where cool drops of dew hang, many-hued jewels
— it's so full of tenderness.

*Pyŏngchon, November 23, 2001*

# 차례
# Contents

## 3부  가상현실
### Virtual Reality

# 1993

## 색동 단풍숲을 노래하라
Sing the many-colored maple groves

# 다듬잇돌

지금도 기억나요 — 어머니
어머니의 젖맛은 참 썼어요
남들은 소태를 발라서 그렇다고 했지만
전 믿지 않았어요 — 다만 어머니 왼쪽 젖 밑에
커다란 흉터 하나 있는 탓이라 생각했어요
그 쓰디쓴 젖, 어쩌자고 저는,
일곱 살 다 되도록 빨았는지요
눈 꽉 감고 소태맛 빨면 그 너머너머 —
엷게 비치던 진짜 젖맛

열 살 때 기미독립 만세소리에 놀란 가슴 —
징용 갔다 병 얻어 온 남편이 있는데,
흙 속에 묻은 가슴 —
그 후 또 난리 터져 북쪽 사람들 내려와
큰아들 데려가 무슨 완장 채우더니
남쪽 사람들 올라와
산으로 끌고 간 뒤 소식 감감한
태산 같은 큰아들
깊이깊이 묻힌 가슴 —
(가슴에 흉터 없으면 조선 어머니 아니어요
조선 땅에 소태맛 아닌 어머니 젖 어디 있겠어요)

16

# A fulling-block

I still remember, mother,
how bitter your milk was.
Some said it was because of the juice you put on your nipples.
I wouldn't believe that — I thought it was all the fault
of the great scar you had below your left breast.
I sucked the bitter milk till I was nearly seven,
I don't know why,
and as I sucked at that bitter taste with eyes tightly closed,
far beyond it came a faint trace of true milk's taste.

When you were ten, that breast was startled —
by the shouts of the Independence Uprising;
that breast buried your husband —
after he came home sick from a Japanese labor camp;
then the Northerners came south armed to destroy,
took away your first son, made him wear an armband,
then the Southerners returned
and dragged up into the hills your rock-like first son.
He was heard of no more,
buried deep in that breast.
(There is never a Korean mother without a scar
on her breast. Every mother's milk tastes bitter in this land.)

해마다 제삿날은 돌아오지만
거미 같은 막내아들 앞세우고 잿밥 올리려니
하늘에 뜬 둥근 달
뻥 뚫린 내 가슴이구나
이담에 이 에미 죽으면 화장해서
뼛가루 임진강 물결에 띄워보내라
산 사람끼리 밥 몇 술 더 나눠먹는 게 옳은 일 같다
울화통에선지 깨우침에선지
제사 같은 것 다 집어치우셨지요
뜨내기 상사手늘, 꽝수리 인 아낙늘, 한사코 붙잡아
토장국 ― 시원한 배추국 ― 끓여 빈 창자 채워주고
손바닥만한 인절미 뜨끈뜨끈 먹여 보내셨지요

어머니 쓰시던 다듬잇돌 지금 안방에 놓여 있어요
한쪽 귀퉁이 떨어져 나간 잿빛 ― 다듬잇돌 보면
어머니 가슴의 흉터가 만져져요
왜 그 흉터는 ― 그리 윤이 나고 ― 매끄러웠는지요
빛나는 새살로 아문 ― 상처들 보면
밤하늘에 뻥 뚫린 달 속으로
들어가시는 어머니 모습 보여요

18

"Every year the day for memorial rites comes around but, alas,
there's only this spider-like last son of mine to make offerings.
The full moon in the sky is like the big hole in my heart.
Later, when I'm dead, burn my body
and scatter my ashes on the waves of the Imjin river.
It's better to share those spoonfuls of rice among the living."
One day, in a fit of anger or from sudden illumination,
you did away with all the ancestral offerings.
Instead, you insisted that travelling vendors stay,
women carrying baskets on their head, and for them
you boiled tasty soup of cabbage and soypaste,
stuffed their empty stomachs
with hot rice cakes big as your hand.

Now, the fulling-block you used sits in my bedroom,
grayish, one corner chipped away — whenever I see it I feel
I am touching the scar on your breast.
Why was that scar so shiny, so smooth?
Whenever I see bright flesh closing a healing wound
I see you, mother, entering the full moon,
a round hole pierced in the night sky.

달빛 한없이 쏟아져 내리는
그 구멍 속으로 들어가면
빛의 바다 - 눈부신 외로움 - 그 너머
넘실대는 젖물결 - 파도 칠 것 같아요
홑겹 베 적삼 촉촉이 땀에 젖어
인절미 떡 목판 머리에 이고
휘적휘적 앞서가시는 어머니 모습 보여요
쪽찐 머리 은비녀 하나 - 제 가슴에 박혀요

Once I follow you into that hole
from which moonlight comes endlessly gushing out,
there's a sea of light — dazzling loneliness — and — beyond
surging billows of milk, maybe, breaking in waves.
Yes, I see you, mother, marching briskly onward before me
in a thin hemp jacket, moist with sweat,
carrying on your head a large wooden bowl
full of rice cakes.
That silver pin holding your hair in a bun pierces my heart.

* Translators' Note: A fulling-block is a flat block of stone on which, in
older days, Korean women would beat newly washed clothes to smoothness
using two short sticks. The sound came to symbolize women's unceasing
pain, endured for the sake of their family.

# 겨울 빈 들 - 거기 숲

하늘 아래
빈 들 -

아득해라
갈 길 -

눈은
내리고 -

나무들 몇 옹기종기
모여 서서
어깨 걸고
웅성웅성 서성거린다

날아가던 하늘 새 몇 마리
발이 시려
맨발이 시려 -

하늘 아래
빈 들 -
무슨 일인가

# Empty winter plains — with groves

Under the sky
empty plains —

the road before me
stretching endless —

snow
falls —

a few trees
close together
shoulder to shoulder
linger and loiter

a few birds flying in the sky
feet cold
bare feet cold —

under the sky
empty plains —
what's wrong?

내려다본다
눈부셔라, 농성하는 나무들

에라 모르겠다
그냥 내려가
깃 틀고 새끼 치니 —

하늘 아래
빈 들 —
띄엄띄엄
작은 숲 이루어
눈 내린다

They look down.
Dazzling bright,
trees close round, protesting.

But they don't give a damn.
They simply fly down
build nests, raise their young —

under the sky
empty plains —
trees grow into groves
here and there.
Snow falls.

# 스카보로 풍경

호수는 은빛으로
가까이서 뒤척이다
분홍빛으로 저물고
겨울 숲 너머 차들은 멀리
불빛으로만 달리고

호숫가에 서 있는 나무들
물 무서운지 선뜻
발 담그지 못하고
둘러서서 서성서성
물 구경만으로 — 키가 크고

여간해서 봄은 오지 않아
병원 굴뚝 연기 오늘도
직각으로 눕고
그 울음소리 천리 길 간다는
세상에서 제일 슬픈 울음의 새
캐나다 붉은 목댕기 들오리는
1$짜리 동전 속에서만 헤엄치는 듯

# Scarborough landscape

Nearby, the lake
is tossing, silver hued.
The daylight is fading now, pink,
and far off beyond the wintery woods cars
are speeding like so many lights.

The trees by the lakeside
stand in a restless circle,
perhaps afraid of the water,
unable to immerse so much as a toe,
and grow tall — just by looking at the water.

Spring has still barely come.
Today as usual the smoke from the hospital chimney
blows horizontally
while the Canadian red-throated duck,
whose call, the saddest in the world,
is said to travel a thousand leagues,
seems only ever to swim in a one-dollar coin.

딸과 엄마가
열두 해 이민생활
아득한 들판에
아물아물
흰 점 꽃으로
흔들리는
사월 마지막 날

A mother and daughter
in their twelfth year of immigrant life
sway
lightly
like tiny white flowers
in dim distant plains.
The last day of April.

# 땡볕

무덤에 가는 날은 늘 땡볕이다
어린 아기로 다시
낮게 잠든 무덤들
무덤에는 숲이 없다
무덤은 늘 땀 타는 풀잎뿐
금잔디 떼장은 아기들 마당
무덤 너머 청청 하늘에
날개 끝에만 무늬
슬쩍 얹어 멋낸
잠자리 몇 마리
무덤에 그늘 떨어지지 않게
바람 그림자로만
함께 놀잔다
잎새 무성한 고춧잎 그늘에
빨간 손가락들 거꾸로 매달려
땅을 가리킨다
무덤에 가는 날은 늘 땡볕이다

# Scorching sun

The sun is always scorching on days we visit the graves.
Graves lie huddled low, sleeping,
babies again.
The graves have no trees standing nearby.
These graves have nothing but grass that burns off sweat,
clumps of golden grass where those babies play.
In the azure sky above the graves
a few dragonflies, their beauty a light patterning
on the tips of their wings, nothing more,
invite us to play with them
simply as shadows of wind
so that no shade falls across the graves.
In the shade of pepper plants' abundant leaves
red fingers hanging upside down point toward the ground.
The sun is always scorching on days we visit the graves.

# 얼음비 온 다음날 아침
### - 최호봉 님을 위하여


하늘에선 분명 빗방울인데
지상 것에 닿는 순간 빗방울들 쩍쩍
강정 얼음으로 깔리는 날
바퀴 미끄러져 목숨 깨지고
발걸음 휘청 곤두박질
팔다리 꺾어지기 쉬운 날
삶과 죽음이 한순간
만나는 때 — 바로 이런 날이라

얼음비 온 다음날
햇빛 눈부신 아침 —
마당의 키 작은 소나무도
숲속의 키 큰 — 참나무, 밤나무, 자작나무
또 무슨무슨 나무도
들판의 말라버린 억새풀마저
마술지팡이에 닿았느냐
죽음 한복판 겨울인데
모두 수정 꽃 피어 반짝반짝
수정 샹들리에 여기저기 쟁강쟁강

# The morning after freezing rain

- For Ch'oi Ho-bong


They were certainly raindrops in the sky
but they turned into a layer of hard shiny ice
the moment they touched the ground.
A day when lives shatter as wheels skid,
when staggering steps slip, head over heels
it's only too easy to break a limb.
A brief moment when life meets death — that kind of day.


The morning after freezing rain.


A glorious morning.
Has some magic wand touched
the small pines in the backyard,
the taller trees in the forest — oaks, chestnuts, silver birches,
and even the dry grasses in the fields?
In the midst of winter death
all are blossoming and glistening with flowers of crystal;
crystal chandeliers clink on this side and that.

귀 간지럽다
살얼음 뒤덮인 가지 끝마다
얼음 녹이며 바알갛게
숨쉬는
저 겨울눈들 ― 새싹들 ―
목숨의 ― 작은 소용돌이들 ―
그 누가 봄 꽃동산 기막히다 하느냐

재난이 축복일 때 있음으로
이 세상 사는 일
가슴 설렌다
쟁강쟁강 ―

The ears resound —
at every branch-tip covered with a thin coat of ice.
There are those winter germs — melting the ice,
breathing scarlet — sprouts
small eddies — of life.
Who says that spring flowerbeds are breathtaking?

Sometimes even misfortune is blessing
and being alive in this world
makes my heart race.
Clink, clink —

# 새벽숲

바람이 쉬고
어둠이 쉬고
첫 햇살이 쉬고
이슬이 내려와
쉬는 숲

새벽잠 깬
방울새 한 마리
키 작은 나무들만
찾아다니며
어서 자라라
어서 자라라
속삭인다

해 뜨기 전에
어서 자라라

# Forest at daybreak

The wind rests,
the darkness rests,
the sun's first rays rest
as dew falls and rests
in the forest.

A red-breasted robin
awake since daybreak
flits from one small tree to another
whispering:
Hurry up and grow,
Hurry up and grow.

Hurry up and grow,
before the sun comes up.

# 소금 시학

너희는 세상에 소금이 되라 —
소금이 되라?

습기 찬 골목길 썩을 것 많은 세상
썩을 것들 못 썩게
네 염통도 내 영혼도
네 욕심도 내 오기도
소금에 푹 절여 자반 만들라?

너희는 세상에 빛이 되라 —
빛이 되라?

세월의 어둠 — 암흑의 역사 —
단칼에 가르는 눈부신 빛이 되라?
뜨겁게 타는 빛 쏘아
빛부셔 — 눈 못 뜰 —
눈부심이거라?

청청한 잎새들
서리 맞은 듯 나자빠져 늘어지게
고갱이 속속들이 소금 뿌려라?

# The poetics of salt

'Be the salt of the world...'
Be salt?

In a world of damp alleys filled with rotting things,
to prevent rotting things from rotting
salt down your heart and my soul,
your desires and my pride
and pickle them?

'Be light for the world...'
Be light?

Light? Breaking at a single blow
the darkness of the times — a history of darkness?
Become dazzling light,
bursting forth in scorching blaze —
blinding eyes?

Sprinkle salt thickly to the very core of each plant
until the fresh green leaves
wilt and droop as if frost-bitten?

그런 말씀 아닐 터라 -
소금 없으면 콩나물도 시금치도 밍밍
제 맛 안 나느니
허공에 빛 - 없는 듯 그득하여 - 비로소
붉은 꽃 붉고 - 푸른 잎 푸르나니
나무들 둥글게 떠오르나니

가슴 가슴 자취 없이 스며드는
빛이 되고 소금 되어
제 맛들 - 제 빛깔들
본래의 그 푸름 - 그 빛남 - 언뜻언뜻
나의 시는 드러내야 하리
나의 시여 - 빛이 되라
세상에 소금이 되라

That cannot be what was meant —
without salt, bean sprouts and spinach are merely insipid,
unable to yield their proper taste;
the light in the sky — filling it though seeming absent —
allows red trees to be red — green leaves green —
and trees to grow up round.

Becoming light and salt
that penetrate every heart quite undetected,
my poems must bring out
the proper taste — the proper color,
the original green — the brilliance of things —
seen and unseen;
therefore, my poems — go and be light,
be salt for the world.

# 1998

## 산은 새소리마저 쌓아두지 않는구나

Why, the hills do not even hoard birdsong

# 가을밤

깜빡 잊었구나
널어놓은 고추를 거둬들여야지
요즈음 가을밤은
별빛도 예전 같지 않다

땡볕에 꼬리 곧추세우고
탱탱히 약이 올랐던 전갈고추들

녀석들 배를 갈라, 황금씨앗
태양의 정자들을, 저기 별빛 흐릿한
전갈자리에 뿌려나볼까
먹다 남은 상한 단무지 같은
달이 뜬다

# Autumn evening

I quite forgot!
I must bring in the red pepper pods I spread out to dry.
These days, even the starlight on autumn evenings
is not a patch on what it used to be.

Scorpion-like pepper pods, gorged with venom,
tails lifted and hardened in the blazing sunlight!

Right, suppose we set about slitting your bellies, little rascals,
and sprinkle your golden seeds, sperm of the sun,
up there in Scorpio, where the stars glimmer dim?
The moon is going down now
like a slice of stale, left-over pickled radish.

# 가을의 경주 들판

경주 들녘에 역사가 길게 누워 있다
눈 감은 지 오래된 그 여인의 가슴에
젖무덤은 아직 풍만하다
잠은 깊으나 젖샘은 마르지 않아
능 속까지 뻗어내린 실뿌리들이
금관에 맺힌 이슬도 빨아올려
금빛 낟알을 익힌다
여인의 가슴에 섬처럼 떠 있는
눈부신 무덤들 사이로
불란서 고속열차가 화살같이
박히리라는 풍문 속에
참새들만 무어라고 지껄이며 날아오른다
황금새떼 바라보는 허수아비의 눈이 아직은
生金빛이다

# The plains of Kyŏngju in autumn

History stretches far aross the plains of Kyŏngju.
The city's a woman who went to her rest long ages ago,
yet her breasts are still buxom.
Deeply she sleeps, yet the milky founts have not run dry
and the fine rootlets piercing down into her royal tomb,
sucking up the dew pearling on her golden crown
bring grain to golden ripeness.
Sparrows fly up chirping
amidst rumors that the French TGV
will soon pierce like an arrow
between the bright burial-mounds
floating there on her breast like islands.
The eyes of the scarecrow
watching the flocks of golden
birds are still a vivid golden hue.

# 강화도

강화섬은 연꽃 같은 섬이다

비석 세우지 말라

꽃 가라앉는다

화력발전소라니!

# Kanghwa Island

Kanghwa Island is like a lotus blossom.

Erect no memorial stone.

The flower is sinking.

A power station! Here?

# 겨울나무

사람들이 옷을 껴입는 겨울에
왜 나무들은 옷을 벗을까

둥근 어깨며 겨드랑이
가지끝 실핏줄까지
청산리 자작나무는 왜 홀랑 드러내는가

눈송이 펄펄 꽃처럼 날리는 한밤중
춤출 수 없는 몸이라면 차라리
꼿꼿이 서서 얼어죽겠다?

깨질 듯한 하늘
찬바람 둥둥한 서슬에
낮달이 썩썩 낫을 가는 속수무책의 대낮,

겁먹고 숨죽인 봄햇살 유혹하려면
어쩌란 말이냐
무등산 겨울나무는 알몸의
신부가 되는 수밖에.

# Winter trees

In winter, when people put more clothes on,
why do the trees take all their clothes off?

Why do the birch trees on the violet hills expose
their rounded shoulders, their armpits,
even the tiny veins at the ends of their branches?

Would they rather stand upright and freeze to death
if they can't move their bodies in dance with the snowflakes
flying flowerlike late at night?

The sky is about to break,
the wind bristles with ice
and the daytime moon sharpens its sickle — a hopeless midday.

What if they were intent
on tempting the fearful, bashful spring sunshine?
Those winter trees on Mudŭng Mountain
have no choice but to be naked brides.

# 겨울새
- 나희덕 시인에게


겨우내 얼지 않는 폭포 뒤쪽 벼랑에서
겨울새 한 마리가 둥지 틀고
맑은 알을 기른다

눈 덮여 가지 휘어진
나무들의 사타구니에도 눈이 소복하다
알들을 품속에서 굴려보는데
몸집 큰 눈덩이가 머리 위에 덮쳐
그를 눈 속에 파묻는다
도리질하는 그의 부리 끝에도
눈가루가 묻어 있다

길 잃은 물방울 몇이서 벼랑 위로 솟구치다가
전속력으로 떨어지는 물방울과
눈보라 속에서 이마받이한다
겨울새의 까만 눈동자에
두 겹의 노란 테가 둘려 있어
폭포의 속도에 금반지를 끼워본다

# Winter bird

A winter bird builds its nest in a cliff
behind a waterfall that stays unfrozen all winter long,
and cherishes one limpid egg.

Snow lies deep in the groins of trees,
their branches bent under burdens of snow.
As she hugs the egg close to her breast
a large ball of snow falls on her head
burying her deep.
As she shakes her head, the tip of her beak
is covered with powdery snow.

A few drops of water, losing their way,
go sprinting up the cliff
and in the driving snow
collide with other drops falling at full speed.
The winter bird's black eyes are rimmed
with a double golden line,
slipping a golden ring on the waterfall's rapidity.

# 그 섬에

끝내 닻을 감지 못했다

자작나무 물오르는 언덕 아래
젊은 무덤 하나 탱탱히 숨죽이고 있다는
너의 해안선
손끝에 퉁겨만 보고
아득히 가지 못했다
지금 눈 내린다

우연의 눈빛
천둥도 없이 마주쳐
황금사과 익어가는
너의 숲속

돛 달고 시퍼런 물살 갈라
눈감고 갔다
눈떠서 오는 그 길

지금 눈 내린다
하늘 버리고 내려와
겨울나무 꼭대기 까치집에도

# To that island

I could not raise the anchor after all.


Merely tapping with a fingertip on your shoreline
where, they say,
a young grave lies tightly holding its breath
below a hill where sap was rising in the birch trees,
I could not go so far.
Now, snow is falling.


A chance glance
met without peals of thunder
ripens golden apples
within your groves.


I took the road toward you with eyes closed,
dividing the bluest waves with sails taut,
and returned open-eyed.


Now, snow is falling.
Descending, leaving the sky behind,
snow is piled high in the magpies' nests

눈은 쌓여, 이 세상
하늘만큼 환한 오늘
돛폭은 바람에 부풀어
출항을 재촉하는데

눈 그친 저녁이면 누군가
저녁해 붉은 빛에
몸 씻으러 나온다는 무덤가
바다가재보다 더 붉은
노을이 탄다
이제 잠행의 밤은 올까

가지 못해
낯익은 물결 너머
가지 않아 눈부신
너의 해안선

at the top of the bare winter trees today
and this world is as bright as the sky.
My sail is eager to leave harbor,
billowing in the wind.

They say when the evening falls and the snow stops,
someone emerges from the grave to bathe
in the crimson rays of the setting sun.
Now at the grave the sunset blazes
redder than any crayfish.
Will the evening come, a stealthy traveler in the dark?

Unable to go,
not having gone,
beyond the familiar waves
so bright, your shoreline.

# 나팔꽃

하늘보다 먼저
하늘빛으로 깨어나

바람결에도
살점 묻어나는
갓난아기 살결이다가

아침 햇살에 힘살 박혔다 싶으면 벌써
이빨 빠진 할머니
오므린 입술이다가

이튿날 새벽보다 앞서
푸른 하늘 깔아놓는
단명한 꽃

지상 것치고
목숨 그리 짧은 것 어디 있으랴

# Morning-glory

Waking earlier than the sky
with the same sky-blue hue,

it's the skin of a new-born babe
which even a breeze might bruise.

By the time the morning sunlight flexes its muscles,
it already has the puckered lips
of an old woman.

Shortlived flower,
spreading out an azure sky
ahead of tomorrow's dawn,

is there anything with so short a life
anywhere on earth?

# 단풍연어

바다를 떠나 강물 거슬러
계곡을 따라 폭포 뛰어넘어

산골 시냇물에
알 낳으러 가자

가는 길 험한 길
오호라, 윗입술 휘어지고
등줄기에 힘살 박혀
온몸에 단풍 든다

심심산골 얕은 여울물
그 바다 자갈돌들 맨몸으로 떼밀어
돌 틈에 알 낳고
모두 함께 세상 뜨자

우리의 여행길은 물결 위에
단풍잎 그득 떠내려가는
전멸의 길

# Autumn-red salmon

Leaving the ocean, heading upstream
following valleys, leaping cascades,

let's go to lay our eggs
in remote mountain streams.

The path we take is a perilous path
alas; with upper lips curled
the muscles clenched along the backbone
our whole body takes on autumn-red tints.

Pushing with naked bodies at the pebbles
at the bottom of shallow brooks deep in the mountains,
let's lay our eggs between the stones
and all together quit this world.

Our journey's path
is a path of annihilation
where countless red leaves go drifting on the waves.

자연의 낭비라 슬퍼 말라
산새들 멧새들 가시 발라
그 죽음 먹어 울음소리 눈부시다

얼음장 돌 틈에서
겨울 지낸 갓난아이들아
수정란에 박아놓은 까만 점
깜박깜박 너희들 눈알이다

봄볕이 왔다
송사리와 장난치며
어미들 왔던 길 되밟아
시퍼런 바다로 떼지어 가라

다시 강물 거슬러
너희들 붉은 알몸
폭포 위에 솟구치지 않는다면
온 산에 어이 단풍 들랴

Do not grieve at nature's so-called prodigality.
Wild birds, mountain birds all pick our bones
and having eaten our death sing dazzling songs.

Little newborn babes that spent the winter
between the ice-coated stones,
the black specks set in the fertilized eggs
are your sparkling eyes.

Now spring sunlight has come.
Go swarming back down the path
your mothers came by, to the deep blue sea,
playing with the minnows along the way.

If your scarlet nakedness
does not again blaze bright far up the stream
above the cascades
how will the mountain blaze bright with autumn-red hues?

# 벌새

줄기 박차고 하늘을 떠도는
너, 모든 꽃들의 꿈

위 아래 앞 뒤 어디로든
날갯짓 자유로운 꽃팔랑개비

낳은 알 콩알만하니
아마 날아다니는 빨간 콩꽃

씨앗들이 일제히
낙하산 타고 날아오르는 숲의 오후
허공에 주삿바늘 같은 부리 박고
송사리 눈 깜박이며
숲을 온통 푸르게 부풀리는 너

호두알만한 둥지 속으로 숨어드는
시속 80km의 푸른 회오리바람

# Hummingbird

You are every flower's dream,
quitting the stem and floating through the air.

Flower-pinwheel freely flying
wherever you will — up, down, forward, backward —

perhaps a flying crimson bean flower
since the eggs you lay are the size of a bean.

You cause the whole forest to swell green,
inserting your needle-like beak into the empty air,
your minnow-like eyes twinkling,
in an afternoon in the forest
when all the seeds fly together into the air on parachutes.

Green whirlwind, sixty miles per hour,
hiding in your nest the size of a walnut.

# 아, 오월

파란불이 켜졌다
꽃무늬 실크 미니스커트에 선글라스 끼고
횡단보도 흑백 건반 탕탕 퉁기며
오월이 종종걸음으로 건너오면

아, 천지사방 출렁이는
금빛 노래 초록 물결
누에들 뽕잎 먹는 소낙비 소리
또다른 고향 강변에 잉어가 뛴다

# Ah, May

The lights have turned green
and as May comes tripping
in a flowery miniskirt and sunglasses, tapping
a brisk rhythm on the black and white keys of the crossing,

ah, swelling round on every side,
the golden songs, the green waves,
the downpour sound of silkworms eating mulberry leaves.
The carp leap in another home village stream.

# 어머니

춘분 가까운 아침인데
무덤 앞 상석 위에 눈이 하얗다

어머님, 손수 상보를 깔아놓으셨군요
생전에도 늘 그러시더니
이젠 좀 늦잠도 주무시고 그러세요
상보야 제가 와서 깔아도 되잖아요

# Mother

On a morning near the spring equinox
the offering-stone before her grave is white with snow.

Why, Mother, you've spread the tablecloth yourself.
That's what you always used to do, of course
but now you should sleep late of a morning.
Can't you let me spread the tablecloth?

* Translators' Note : An offering-stone is the low slab of stone in front of
a grave, on which offerings of food and drink are placed when the family
comes to pay its respects to the dead.

# 연꽃

　이별의 신비


연꽃봉오리
부풀리고 자취 없는 손길
어디 있을까

꽃봉오리 젖꼭지엔 아직 젖은 진흙
지문도 또렷한데
내일 꽃송이 벌어질 때

맑게 손 씻고
물밑에서
올려다보고 있을까 그이는

바람결에 등만 보여줄 꽃송이
수면에 캄캄하리
꽃 그림자

스스로 눈부시거라
이젠 타인의 몸

# A lotus

Mystery of separation


Where is that hand
that has brought the lotus blossom swelling
then left without a trace?

Fingerprints are clear
in the still moist clay on the budding nipple
and tomorrow, when the flower opens wide,

he may gaze up
from under the water,
hands washed translucent.

The blossom will show only its back in the wind.
the shadow of the flower
will be dark on the water.

Be bright by yourself.
You're another's body now.

# 연잎

## 만남의 신비


떠돌이 빗방울들 연잎을 만나
진주알 되었다

나의 연잎은 어디 계신가,

나는 누구의 연잎일 수 있을까

# Lotus leaves

### Mystery of meeting

Meeting lotus leaves,
wandering raindrops have turned into pearls.

Where can I find my own lotus leaf?

Whose lotus leaf can I be?

# 이삿날

이삿짐 나가고
텅 빈 방이
말할 때마다
우르르르 울린다

품고 있던 자식들
하나 둘 날아가면
깃털 몇 개 흩어진
가슴속 빈 마루만
우르르르 울리려니

귀뚜라미, 흰눈썹황금새
모두 사라지고
대동강, 다뉴브강의 푸른 물결
꺼멓게 썩어
지상에 사람만 남고
잉어와 메기도 철새 따라
흰 구름 너머 이사간 날
지구는 메아리도 없이
우르르르 어이 우나

# Moving away

Once the furniture's gone
each time I speak
the empty room
rings with a trembling echo.

When cherished children
leave the nest one by one,
the empty floor of my heart
where a few feathers lie scattered
will ring with a trembling echo.

On the day crickets and goldfinches
all vanish,
and the blue waters of Daedong and Danube,
rotting, turn black,
when only people are left in the world
while carp and catfish follow migrant birds
away beyond the white clouds,
how could the earth cry trembling,
when there's no echo left?

# 잠자리의 노래

날개 끝자락
수면에 닿을 듯 드리우고
구름 보며 넋없이 앉아 있는데
허리께로 출렁이는 손길

파르르
날아올라 - 뒤돌아보니
목마름 넘치는 호수 물결

당신이 날 만졌잖아요

물속 기어다니던
어린시절 지나가고
탈바꿈의 캄캄한 별밤 건너
맑은 당신 눈동자에
갓 펼친 날개 비추어보던 첫날
당신은 내 날개가
성당의 색유리 무늬 같다고
놀라면서 바라보셨지요

저녁놀은 불타고
목마름은 넘쳐
바람도 없는데

# Song of a dragon-fly

The wing tips
dipping low as if about to touch the water,
it perches gazing absently at the clouds in the sky
then a hand comes rippling toward its waist.

Zooming upward
looking back —
it was the waves of the lake overflowing with thirst.

You touched me!

Once my infant days
under water were past,
on the first day when I met these freshly unfolded wings
in your clear eyes
you said, gazing in amazement,
"Your wings are like the patterns in
church stained-glass windows."

The sunset is glowing,
thirst overflowing,
no hint of breeze

출렁이는 당신의 눈동자

목마름 모르던 이 몸
오늘 이렇게 당신 출렁이니
당신 물가에 더욱 가고 싶어
날개가 떨려요

당신이 날 만졌기 때문이어요

꼬리끝 물속에 담그고
당신 기슭에 내려앉을 날
내일인가요
어제였나요

your eyes flow in waves.

I have never known thirst
but seeing you flowing like this today
my wings tremble
with a desire to go near your shore
because you have touched me.

When can I settle at your edge
and dip the tip of my tail in the water —
tomorrow?
yesterday?

# 탄생

아내의 자궁에 아기가 들어선 날
죽음도 함께 따라와 누웠다
죽음이 하얀 달걀만큼 자랐을 때
내 아기는 오리알만큼 커 있었다

어느날 초음파로 잡은 아내의
자궁 속 어두운 바다 수평선에
달걀이, 아아, 달같이 지고

오리알에서 아기가
우주인처럼 기어나온다

하혈의 저녁놀 너머
먼동을 향해
내 아들이 밤새워 유영을 한다

# Birth

The day the baby entered my wife's womb
death followed it and settled there too.
When death had grown as big as a white hen's egg
my baby was the size of a duck's egg.

One day on the shore of the dark ocean
inside my wife's womb, caught by ultrasound,
there was the hen's egg, ah, setting like the moon

and out of the duck's egg the baby
was emerging like an extraterrestrial.

Beyond the evening glow of issuing blood
my son was swimming on through the night
toward distant daybreak.

# 푸른 새

막막한 우주 공간은
물살 거센 암흑의 바다

방사선 자외선 적외선이
세찬 물결 이루어 출렁이는 거기
돛단배처럼 푸른 혹성 하나 떠 있다

그 별에서 날아오르는 비둘기 한 마리
사방은 검푸른 물결뿐 앉을 곳 없다

불현듯 회오리바람 불어오면,
그 별 어디엔가 숨어 있을 맑은 샘
뜨거운 모래 속에 금세라도 파묻힐 듯

그러나 무서운 침묵의 우주 심연 뚫고
생명의 푸른 별이 작은 새처럼 날아갈 때
시간과 공간이 물비늘을 턴다

이 작은 새의 붉은 가슴에
독침을 꽂고 있는 우리는 누구인가

# Blue bird

The vast expanse of empty space
is a sea of darkness rough with waves.

Radioactive, ultraviolet and infrared rays
arise and surge in fierce waves, and there
floats one blue planet like a small sailing ship.

A single dove flying up from that planet
finds nowhere to settle but those dark blue waves.

It seems the clear spring hidden somewhere on that planet
will be buried in no time under the hot sand
when a sudden whirlwind rises

but as that blue planet of life passes, piercing
the fearful silence of the cosmic abyss like a little bird,
time and space shake off scales of water.

Who are we, who pierce
that little bird's crimson breast with poisoned darts?

# 2001

## 가상현실
Virtual reality

# 수술

1
벌거벗은 몸 환자복에 담겨
새벽 6시 45분에 입원실을 떠난다
누운 채 하얀 관 같은 승강기 속으로 떠밀려
지하로 떨어진 뒤, 이마 위로 빠르게 스치는
천장의 형광등 불빛 따라 긴 복도 꺾이고
또 꺾이고 이윽고 도착한 냉동실 비슷한 곳,
참 먼 곳 수술실은 싸늘하다.
수술대로 옮겨 뉘어지고, 이내 내 영혼은
낯선 길을 떠난다.

2
여기가 어디인가

가만히 내려다보니
누구네 집 마당에 잔치가 한창인데
푸른 옷에 푸른 마스크 쓴 사람들
수군대는 소리
술이 떨어졌다는 얘기가 들리고

86

# The operation

1

At 6:45 in the morning I leave the ward,
my naked body shrouded in a hospital gown.
Lying flat, I am pushed into an elevator like a white coffin;
we fall to the basement, follow the light from lamps
in the ceiling that quickly brush past above my brow;
the corridor turns,
turns, and finally arrives in a place like a freezer,
a far away place. The operating room is cool.
I am moved to the operating table, installed there;
in a flash my soul sets off
on a journey to an unfamiliar land.

2

Where am I?

On careful inspection, a party
seems to be in full swing in the yard of someone's house,
people in green robes with green masks,
whispering voices,
someone can be heard saying that they've run out of wine

은백색 형광 햇빛 떨어지는
인적 없는 뒷마당에는
물동이 여섯 개쯤 놓여 있다

아득히 먼 나라에 혼자 와서
뒤뜰의 고요에 더럭 겁이 날 때
어디선가 두런대는 목소리

얘야, 이 집에 포도주가 떨어졌다
여인이여, 나와는 상관없는 일입니다

갈비뼈 빗장 열고 핏빛 대문으로 들어온
푸른 마스크 푸른 옷 입은 사람들이
바쁘게 오가며
물항아리에 물을 채운다

3
고통은 그 자체가 하나의 발광체, 찬란해라,
모르핀으로도 잠들지 않는 그 별빛 따라
갈 때와는 다른 길로 병실에 돌아온다
여덟 시간 만의 귀환, 귀향은 늘 새로운 아픔인데
그 항아리 물들 포도주로 변했을까

while in the deserted backyard
where a silvery fluorescent sunlight is falling
half-a-dozen water jars have been put ready.

I am on the verge of panic at the silence in the back garden,
alone here in this far-away country,
when I hear voices murmuring:

Child, this family has run out of wine.
Woman, that has nothing to do with me.

The people wearing green robes and green masks
have slid back rib-bolts and entered through blood-red gates.
Now they are coming and going busily,
filling the jars with water.

3
Pain is its own luminosity, shining oh so bright.
Following it comes a starlight that no morphine can dim.
I return to the ward by another route than when I went.
Back after eight hours; returning home always brings new pain,
I wonder if the water in those jars has changed into wine?

# 수술 이후


허파 한쪽 잘라낸 후

추수 끝난 논바닥에 괸 물 속

붕어처럼

모로 누워서 흘끗

석양 비낀 하늘 한쪽 곁눈질한다

구름장 시꺼멀수록

      저녁놀은 어기여차 더욱 붉더라

# Post-operational

One whole section of a lung removed,

I squint sideways at a patch of sunset sky

like a carp

lying aslant

stranded in a stagnant pool in a harvested paddy-field.


The blacker the clouds are

        the brighter the twilight glows — cheery.

# 아픈 장미

### Blake 풍으로


폭풍의 밤에 길 잃은
벌레 한 마리
오두막 불빛 보고, 아 —
네 품속 파고들었다

진홍빛 침대에 누워
한 밤 푹 자고 가게
창문은 열어두렴
겁내지 마라
곧 동이 튼다, 장미야

# The sick rose

### After William Blake

Losing its way one stormy night
a worm
glimpsed light from a hovel
and burrowed into your breast.

Leave the window open
and let it sleep a good night's sleep
on your crimson bed.
Do not be afraid, rose.
Day will soon break.

# 회복 예감

뺨 간질여주고
팔뚝 깨물어주고 싶은
포동포동
아기비 내리네

봄햇살 엮어 유록색 발을 내린
수양버들 사이로
볼기짝 살짝 때려주고 싶은
옹알옹알
아기비 내리네

불치병 선고받고 겨울 난 뒤
봄비 내리는 날

# Signs of recovery

Infant raindrops fall
plump and round.
I long to tickle their cheeks
and nibble at their arms.

Infant raindrops fall
murmuring.
I long to spank them lightly
through the yellow-green screen of weeping willows
woven with rays of spring sunshine.

A day of spring rain —
a winter has passed since I was pronounced incurable.

# 난처한 늦둥이

새벽 아득한 잠결에 누군가 얼굴을 더듬는다
　　아내의 손길이 턱수염을 만지작거리고
　　눈썹을 문질러보고 오른쪽 눈두덩 아래
　　검버섯도 쓸어본다
나는 눈을 꼭 감고 숨을 죽인다
　　　　아내의 손길이 더듬는 것
　　스물다섯 해 우리들이 함께한
　　　　　　이 세상 소풍 이야기일까
　　　　검버섯 뒤에 피어나는
　　　　심연의 적막일까
　　잠자는 척 눈감고 있다가
　　실눈을 뜨고 보니
아내의 눈도 감겨 있다
아내의 손길이 더듬어 달래고 있는 것
　　싸늘한 형광불빛 아래
　　내가 여덟 시간 동안
　　발가벗겨져 뉘어졌던 사건 이래
　　　어이없게도 우리들 이불 속으로
　　　파고 들어와 새근새근 잠들어 있는
　　갓난 죽음, 아내는 이 늦둥이가
깨어나 칭얼댈까 겁이 나는 것일 게다

# Awkward lateborn

In the vague sleep of dawn I feel someone touching my face.
My wife's hand fumbles at my chin
rubs my eyebrows, brushes across the dark spot
under my right eye.
I keep my eyes shut and hold my breath.
Is the touch of my wife's hand
telling me something about the twenty-five years
of the outing through life we have shared
or the desolation of the abyss blossoming
behind the dark spot?
Having kept my eyes shut pretending to sleep,
I open them slightly
and find that my wife's eyes are shut too.
What my wife's hand touches and caresses
is the new-born death that came
burrowing absurdly and now sleeps quietly
under our bedclothes
after I was laid naked
for eight hours
under cold fluorescent lights.
Perhaps she fears
her late-born infant will wake and cry.

•

97

아내여, 마음 졸이지 마오
안 나오는 젖이나마 물려주고
둥기둥기 업어주다 보면
혹시 누가 아오, 그 녀석 순둥이로 자라 효도할지

Wife dear, don't be troubled.
If you feed it at your dry breast
and carry it gently on your back
who knows, the infant may grow up a dutiful child.

# 그믐께

버드나무 이웃에 놔두고
고압선철탑 위에
까치집이 얹혀 있다
맵찬 겨울바람에
버드나무 가지들 부르르
온몸 떠는 초저녁

그믐달이 까치집을
기웃이 들여다본다
얼기설기 바구니 속
얼마나 추울까

곧 떠나야 할 먼 겨울 뱃길이
두려운 나는 고개 길게 빼고
슬쩍 들여다본다
백자접시 그믐달에
무엇이 담겼나

불가해한, 별무늬 그믐밤
고압전류 흐르는
아, 호기심조차 눈감아버린, 칠흑어둠

# Waning moon

Although there is a poplar tree nearby,
a magpie has perched its nest
on a high-voltage pylon.
It's early evening
and all the poplar's branches are shaking
in the bitter winter wind.

The waning moon glances sideways
into the nest.
How cold it must be
in that basket with its many holes.

Dreading the long winter journey ahead
I crane my neck
and look up furtively.
What might the waning moon's
white porcelain bowl contain?

Inscrutable, the waning moon's star-patterned night,
high voltage flowing,
ah, curiosity itself has closed its eyes — pitch black darkness.

아니! 얇은 껍질 살짝 쪼개면, 흰 속살
눈부실, 가짓빛 밤의, 매혹

No! Egg-plant-hued night's seduction — dazzling —
will be the white flesh within,
once the brittle shell cracks open.

# 가상현실

암선고를 받은 순간부터
(암은 언제나 진단이 아니라 선고다)
너의 세상은 환해진다
컴퓨터 화면 위를 떠도는 창문처럼
기억들이 날아다닌다
원시의 잠재의식도 살아나서
뚜벅뚜벅 걸어오고, 저 우주에 있는 너의 미래의
별똥들이 쏟아진다
어둠은 추방되고, 명암도 무늬도 사라진,
두께도 깊이도 무게도 지워진,
노숙과 밥굶기와 편안한 잠과 따뜻한 한 끼의
경계가 무너지고, 모든 칸막이가 허물어진
환하디 환한 나라
시간의 뿌리와 공간의 돌쩌귀가
뽑혀나간 너의 현실은 안과 밖 따로 없이
무한복제로 자가 증식하는
아, 디지털 테크놀로지 최첨단
암세포들의 세상
지독한 오염 환경에서 살아남을 수 있는
미국자리공, 황소개구리, 실지렁이, 거머리가 못 되어
시름시름 힘을 잃고 약자로 전락한 어느 순간부터

# Virtual reality

From the moment you receive a cancer verdict
(cancer is always a verdict, not a diagnosis)
your world brightens up.
Memories fly about
like the windows revolving on a screen saver.
The subconscious of a primitive age wakes up
and comes strutting by, while meteors
flash down from your future up in space.
Darkness banished, light and shade, patterns removed,
thickness, depth and weight abolished,
differences between living on the street with starvation
and a snug bed at home with warm meals obliterated,
all demarcations destroyed,
world of clear bright light.
With the roots of time and the stone hinges of space
eliminated, your reality becomes
a world of cancerous cells,
self-reproducing limitlessly
without distinction between inside and out,
oh, the very height of digital technology,
caught in the trap of a restructuring
designed to weed out the uncompetitive
at the very instant when,
incapable of surviving amidst toxic conditions,
unlike pokeweed, bullfrogs, threadworms, leeches,
they have little by little lost their vitality,

경쟁력 없는 자 솎아버리는 구조조정의
덫에 걸린 너의 삶은
순백색 빛의 나라, 가상현실

declined into weakness, your life,
a world of pure white light, virtual reality.

# 맑다가 흐린 날

구름 한 점 없더니
어느새 흐린 하늘입니다
유카리나무 밑에 잠들었던
강물이 다시 출렁입니다

흠뻑 젖은 날개 햇볕에 바싹 말려
빨래처럼 탁탁 털어 접고
가마우지 한 마리가 물 속으로
사라집니다 오랜 잠수 끝에
치켜든 그의 부리 끝에서 은빛 물고기
알몸으로 눈부시게 꿈틀댑니다

강물은 별빛 흉내내며 흐르고
바람결에 나뭇잎들은
물결 흉내내며 반짝입니다
창조 닷샛날 같은 서부호주 백조강변에
엿샛날 처음 눈 뜬 사람처럼
한 달을 살았습니다
천국낙원도 한 달이면
늙은 조강지처인가 봅니다

# Clouds after clear skies

Not a cloud in sight,
then suddenly the sky clouds over.
The river asleep below a eucalyptus tree
undulates, moves on again.

After drying out its soaked wings in the sun
then shaking them thoroughly, folding them up
like laundered clothes,
a cormorant disappears into the water.
After a long submersion,
a silver fish squirms in dazzling nakedness
at the tip of its uplifted beak.

The river flows, mimicking starlight and
the leaves shimmer in the breeze,
mimicking the waves.
I have been living for a month beside Swan River
in West Australia, a place like the world on the Fifth Day,
like the first man
who opened his eyes on the Sixth Day of Creation.
But its seems that after a month, even Paradise
grows as familiar and staid as an aging, long-time wife.

오래된 강물을 하염없이
들여다보다가 어린 물결들의
떠들썩한 소리 옆에 끼고 다시 발길 옮기면
저만치 붉은 댕기머리 찰랑이며 다정히
손잡고 걸어가는 삶과 죽음의
뒷모습 황홀합니다

After gazing blankly at the ancient river, I set off again,
listening to the boisterous chatter of youthful waves.
I see from behind
Life and Death walking hand in hand, affectionately,
red hair-ribbons streaming in the breeze,
a ravishing sight.

# 별똥

죽음에도 울음이 터지고
탄생에도 울음이 터진다

남들을 울리며 떠나는 것이 죽음이라면
탄생은 스스로 울면서 올 뿐
삶의 끝과 시작에는 늘
눈물이 있다

캄캄한 하늘
칠흑의 어둠 가르며
별똥눈물 떨어진다
아, 갑자기 환해지는 마음

누가 죽었나

누가 태어났나

# Meteor

Death brings a burst of tears
and birth a burst of tears.

A departure that makes others cry is death,
birth is a coming at which we ourselves cry;
at the end and beginning of life
there are always tears.

Meteor tears fall
flashing across the black sky,
the pitch-black darkness.
Oh, a sudden illumination touches my heart.

Has someone died?

Has someone been born?

# 껍질 얇은 달팽이

급류무당개구리는 맨날
껍질 얇은 달팽이가 만만한 먹이 같아
냉큼 삼켰다가
맛이 영 형편없어
얼굴 찡그리고 얼른
뱉어버린다
계곡물 곤두박질치는 벼랑끝 나뭇잎에
이슬처럼 매달린 나
개구리가 목구멍 속에서 방금 게워낸
달팽이라면 엄청 좋겠다

달팽이는 세월아 네월아
오늘도 아주 느림보
맛도 별로

# Thin-shelled snails

Every day a red-bellied frog living in the rapids
gulps down
thin-shelled snails thinking they're good to eat
then quickly spits them out
with a grimace
having found they taste awful.
I'm clinging like a drop of dew to a leaf
at the edge of a cliff where the river rushes by.
I wish I were that snail just vomitted up
from the frog's gullet.

The snail is very slow today, as ever,
heedless of the passage of time,
and its taste is nothing special, too.

# 불꽃놀이

이 무슨 난데없는
불꽃놀이냐
이 내 몸뚱이 가운데토막에
무슨 큰 경사라도 난 모양이다
왼쪽 옆구리에서 초저녁에 폭죽 하나
눈부시게 치솟더니,
등허리를 돌아 오른쪽에서도
폭죽 치솟아 여기저기서
기어이 불꽃들 꽝꽝 터진다
연 사흘 한 주일을 밤낮없이 지칠 줄도 모르고
계속되는 통증의 불꽃놀이
몸의 한복판을 찢어 열어 놓은
아픔의 신천지
통증의 강고한 철권정치
아, 아픔 없는 나라에 살고 싶어라
암세포들의 완전 입성을 축하하는 잔치인가
힘줄 한 올 한 올
살점 한 점 한 점
환하게 밝히며
백골의 갈피갈피마다
시나브로 흩날려 쌓이는 송이송이 불꽃

# Fireworks

What are these sudden
fireworks?
Some happy event must have occurred
in the middle of my body.
A petard went soaring up early in the evening,
dazzling bright in my left side;
circling my waist another petard
shot up in my right side, then here and there, everywhere
fireworks started going off.
Fireworks of pain, non-stop
for three days, a week, day and night, tireless,
a new world of suffering
wrenched open in the center of my body,
an iron-fisted rule of pain.
Oh, I wish I were in a land of no pain.
Are they for a triumphal feast
celebrating cancerous cells' capture of my body?
Muscles, fiber by fiber,
flesh, bit by bit,
cluster after cluster of fire-flowers
flutter down little by little, pile up
in every gap of my skeleton.

떨어지는 불꽃 눈부시지만
새로 치솟는 불꽃 더욱 찬란하구나
하늘의 별들을 우러러
몸부림치며 기도를 올리려 하나
악문 어금니라 입술조차 열리지 않는구나
통증은 스스로 눈부신 발광체
뼈마디 마디가 참숯이 되어 내 몸뚱이
가운데 토막에 잉걸불 탄다 한 달 이상 지속되는
무지막지한 이 불길 속에
무슨 비늘 같은
새 생명이라도 하나 벼려낼 수 없을까
진땀 방울 영롱히 까무러치는
아, 황홀한 불꽃놀이
진통(陣痛)이거라
진통이거라

Falling fire-flowers are splendid but
more splendid still those newly blooming.
I struggle to say some words in prayer
gazing up at the stars in the sky
but my clenched molars won't even let my lips open.
Pain is its own luminosity.
Every bone turns to charcoal and burns,
a brazier-full in the middle of my body
for a month and more.
How could I forge
a new life,
even tiny as a needle's point,
in these savage flames?
Oh, could these magnificent fireworks
where drops of sweat fall, swooning pearls,
be labor pains?
May they be labor pains.

# 마니피카트* 1

이 절망, 이 캄캄한 억지
받아들이라니
받아들이라니
암환자의 두려움이 이만할까
죽음의 선고를 받아들이라니

얼마나 겁났을까
얼마나 겁났을까
처녀의 몸으로 사생아를 낳으라니

체념으로, 오기로
불안한 기대로
될 대로 되라지(Let it be) 했더니
그 절망 모르는 사람들은 말하네
지혜로운 순명이었다고

말기 암환자의 절망이 낳은
천지개벽의 꿈으로
불러보는 노래 Magnificat
내 영혼이 내 영혼이
당신을 찬양하며 기뻐합니다

* 마리아의 노래. 누가복음 1장 46절-55절.

120

# Magnificat 1

I am bidden to accept
bidden to accept
this despair, this dark compulsion.
Is this what a cancer patient's fear is like?
Bidden to accept a death sentence?

How frightened she must have been,
how frightened
as she, a virgin, was bidden to bear a bastard.

She said, 'Fiat'
with resignation, with dignity,
with uneasy expectancy,
and those who have never known despair
call it devout obedience.

Magnificat - the song sung
as a dream of new heavens, new earth,
born of the despair of a terminal cancer patient,
my soul, my soul
praises you in joy.

* *Magnificat* is the first word of the Song of Mary in Latin (Luke 1:46-55).

# 마니피카트 3

늦은 밤 강가에
아무도 없습니다
나무 밑 벤치에 달빛이
가만히 내려와 앉습니다
강물 위로 달빛이
슬며시 내려와 눕습니다
누운 달빛과 앉은 달빛이
서로를 바라봅니다
강물 옆에 병든 이 몸도 누워봅니다
온몸이 물소리를 내면서
어디론가 흘러갑니다
언제 어디서나
가득가득 숨죽여
넘치시는 당신
그곳 산모퉁이 강물
일렁이거든 물결 속에
손 담가 더듬어 이 몸 만져지거들랑
당신 것으로 취하소서
영혼으로 능히 육신을
잉태시키시는 임이시여

# Magnificat 3

There is no one
beside the river late at night.
Moonlight drops down quietly
and sits on the bench under a tree.
Moonlight stealthily drops down
and reclines on the river.
The reclining moonlight and the sitting moonlight
contemplate one another.
Beside the river this sick body of mine likewise reclines.
My whole body goes flowing off somewhere,
making a sound like that of water.
With bated breath
ever, everywhere,
you are brimming over.
When the river in that mountain ridge stirs and ripples
dip your hand into the stream, touch me
and take me for your own, I pray.
You, who so easily make bodies
pregnant by soul.

# 탈옥수의 기도

나 이제 도망치리
남회귀선 아래 옛 유형지로
먼 나라 낯선 하늘 아래
땡볕 타는 붉은 사막 위에
맨발로 맨몸으로 서서
세찬 불바람 외면치 않으리

백년해로 유혹하는
항암주사의 치마꼬리 뿌리치고
감히 당신의 몸 받아 먹어
이 몸 안에 모시고
헌 살(肉)의 울타리 훌쩍
월담한 죄인
남십자성 별빛 등에 지고
탈옥의 첫 밤을 맞이하리

꼬리 치켜든 전갈자리별
방사선 눈빛 번뜩이며 추격할 때
아, 임이시여, 이 몸 업어다
강변 풀밭에 다시 뉘어 숫총각 삼아주오

# A jail-breaker's prayer

Now I'll run away
to some old penal colony below the Tropic of Cancer.
In a distant land under foreign skies,
standing barefoot, naked
on a crimson desert under a scorching sun,
I'll not shun the fierce fiery wind.

Rejecting the trailing skirts of anti-cancer drugs
tempting me to grow old with them,
daring to receive your Body
within my body,
a sinner who has leapt over the wall
of his tattered body,
I'll face my first night as a jail-breaker
bearing the Southern Cross on my back.

When Scorpio with its tail raised
comes chasing me, with eyes of flashing radiation,
ah, Love, carry me on your back,
lay me down on the meadow by the river once more
and turn me into a virgin youth.

# 눈초리

나 세상 뜨는 날

고대 이집트인의 얼굴이고 싶다

성벽에, 물병에

새겨져

확신에 찬 눈초리로

지평선 너머

영원을 응시하는

# A look

The day I leave the world

I want to be an ancient Egyptian's face.

Carved

on a city wall or a water-jar,

a look full of certainty

gazing toward eternity

beyond the horizon.

# 오늘의 예언자는

오늘날의 예언자는 누구인가

물이 썩었다고
쌀에 독이 들었다고 짜장면에도 라면에도 국화빵에도
유전자조작 밀가루가 스며들어 있다고
공기에 독극물이 숨어 있다고
내장재 바닥재에 환경호르몬이 잠복해 있다고
우리나라에서 유통되는 정체불명 화학물질
3만7천 종에 2억3천만 톤에 이른다고
이 가운데 유독물 유통량 해마다 100만 톤씩 늘어난다고
살충제 농약 배기가스 제초제로
우리들의 살림터 속고갱이까지 썩었다고
전자파가 어린 뇌세포 서서히 죽이고 있다고

광야에서 외치는 오늘의 선지자는
유방암, 폐암, 대장암, 혈액암, 간암 선고받은
모든 암환자들이다
일급수 아니면 살지 못하는
산천어 열목어 같은 암환자들이야말로
오늘의 이사야, 예레미아이다.

# Today's prophets

Who might today's prophets be?

Proclaiming that the water's polluted;
there's poison in the rice; genetically modified wheat
has got into the Chinese noodles, the ramen and cookies;
there are toxic chemicals hidden in the air; there are
environmental hormones concealed in walls and flooring;
unidentified chemical substances circulating in this country
come to 230 million tons of 37,000 different kinds;
those that are toxic increase by a million tons each year;
the very heart of this land we inhabit
is rotten with pesticides, fertilisers, exhaust fumes, herbicides;
electronic radiation is gradually killing infant brain cells.

The prophets crying in the desert today
are all those who have been condemned to cancer —
of the womb, the lungs, the intestine, the blood, the liver —
cancer patients, sure not to survive unless in purest water,
like trout or salmon,
are today's Isaiah, Jeremiah.

# 퍼스, 2000년 새해


흐르는 세월에 금을 그어
새천년 새해가
밝아왔다고 난리들이다
　　적도 너머
　　　　남회귀선도
　　　　　　　　한참 지나온 이곳
연일 39도를 넘나드는 폭서의 땡볕인데
북쪽 고향은
　　　　혹한의 정월

어느 정초 살얼음 낀
강변을 걷다 보니
　　　　흰 물새가 긴 부리로 끼룩끼룩
　　　　　　　　은빛 물고기를 통째로 삼키고 있었지
귀때기 얼어터지는 새해 며칠
맨 몸으로 떨고 있는 강가의 미루나무들
　　　　　　강물 건너 모래톱을
　　　　뒤덮은 하얀 새똥
꿈틀대던 생명의 흰 점 기억들

# Perth, New Year's Day 2000

People draw an arbitrary line across the flow of time
and declare that the first new year
of a new millennium has dawned.
      Here in Perth,
              far from the Equator,
                    and from the Tropic of Capricorn,
it is sun-scorched, 39 degrees every day,
while back home far to the north
      January is icy cold.


Early one January, walking
by a lightly frozen river
      I saw a white water bird with a long beak
              swallow whole a silver fish.
A few days into the ear-freezing new year
poplar trees were trembling naked on the river bank,
        white bird-droppings covered
      a sandbar across the river —
white-speckled memories of writhing life.

한반도의 겨울 해는
노루 꼬리만큼
　　　　길어지고,
하지 지난 이곳은
캥거루 귀만큼
　　　　길어진 밤,

회청색 유카리나무 잎새 사이로
날개치며 하얗게 날아오르는 것
　　고향 강변 떠나온
　　　　　　　겨울 물새들이냐
　　　　미래의 기억 속
은빛 물고기떼들이냐

인도양과 남극해가
만나며 갈라지는
암사자 봉(Cape Leeuwin) 앞바다 파도 속으로
20세기의 마지막 햇살이 묻힌다

오랜만에 큰 눈 내렸다는 목포 해안
남해 물결 서해 물결 철썩철썩 몸 섞으며

The winter days in the Korean peninsula
have lengthened by as much
                as a deer's tail
while here the nights since the solstice
have lengthened
                by as much as a kangaroo's ear.


Some white forms wing their way up
flapping among the gray-blue eucalyptus leaves —
            are they wintering birds
                    from the rivers back home?
              or swarms of silver fish
from memories to come?


The last sun of the twentieth century has been laid to rest
in the waves off Cape Leeuwin
where the Indian Ocean and the Antarctic Ocean
meet and divide


And this evening off Mokpo where the first snow in years
has fallen, the waters of the Southern Sea

이 밤도 핥고 있겠지, 수북이 쌓인 그 팥빙수
　　　동지와 하지가 불현듯
같은 날이고
　　　불타던 내일 하루도
남십자성 별빛 아래

　　　가짓빛 밤으로 새삼 저물리라
달빛 환한 어린 시절 풀섶
둥지 속 알들의 따뜻한 침묵을 품고
호주대륙 서남단 강변을 서성이는 이 유신은

　　　어느 날개 달린 새해의 기억일까

and the Western Sea must be mingling,
slurping and lapping at a mound of bean sherbet ice.
　　　　Winter solstice and summer solstice
suddenly fall on the same day
　　　　and sun-scorched tomorrow
will set anew into egg-plant tinted night


　　　　　　　　beneath the stars of the Southern Cross.
Nestling in the warm silence of eggs hidden in long grass
in my moonlit childhood's nest
loitering along a south-west Australian riverside,


which memories of winged new years are this body of mine?

# 감사 예절

호주 토인들은
도대체 감사할 줄 모른다
비스킷, 초콜릿 몇 개 주고
코카콜라 몇 깡통 주고
고맙다는 인사
아예 기대도 말 일이다

호주 원주민들에게는
모든 것은 부족의 신들이 주는 것
매년 모여 춤과 노래로
신들에게 감사하면 그만이다

만인이 같은 부족의 형제자매인데
하늘 아래 모든 것 네 것이고 내 것인데
누가 누구에게 감사한단 말인가
거저 주고 거저 받을 뿐
고맙다는 말을 모른다
인간에게 감사하는 예절 아예 없으니
배은망덕도 없는,
무지개뱀의 검은 후손들
아, 황홀한 야만 ―

# Formalities of thanks

Native Australians
do not know how to say thanks.
If you give them biscuits or some chocolate,
or a few cans of coca-cola,
you must not expect
any kind of expression of thanks.

To Australian aborigines
everything is a gift from their tribal spirits.
Once a year they gather to thank the gods
in songs and dances, and that is all.

We are all brothers and sisters of the same tribe,
everything under the heavens is yours and mine,
so no need to say thanks to anyone.
All is freely given, freely received,
and as there's no word for thanks
there's no ingratitude either.
Ah, how fascinating the barbarity
of the black descendants of the Rainbow Serpent!

하늘 아래 새로운 것 아무것도 없는데
땅 위에 새롭지 않은 것 하나도 없는데
특허권, 저작권, 온갖 기득권
신성불가침으로 떠받드는
아, 징그러운!
선진문명의 예의 바른 율법.

There's nothing new under the sun
and there's nothing in the world that is ever old
so how disgusting
the laws of etiquette in advanced civilizations
that consider patents, copyrights, and vested rights
sacred and inviolable.

# 새벽 강물

오늘도 강변을 걷는다
바다가 가까운 이 강에는
정한수 떠놓고 무릎 꿇고
천지신명께 빌고 있는
새벽 강물

물결 모양 심상치 않아
유심히 살펴보니
등지느러미 끝 적시는 첫 햇살로
물살 서늘히 가르며
내 마음속 깊이
잠수하는 돌고래 두 마리

물결은 발밑 풀섶에 출렁이고
하늘의 어느 물가 떠나
밤새워 날아온 펠리칸들이
날개 접고 맨살의 긴 부리로
내 가슴속 수심도 재고 있다
아, 선명해라
물거울에 비치는 펠리칸 그림자

# Early morning river

Today again I walk beside the river.
In this river, close to the sea,
the water kneels at dawn in deep meditation
invoking the god of heaven and earth


Odd ripples out in the stream —
I look more closely —
two dolphins cleave the waves smoothly,
the first rays of the sun drenching their dorsal fins,
and plunge deep into my heart.


The wavelets ripple against the bed of reeds at my feet;
pelicans that have flown all night long
from some heavenly shore
fold their wings and fathom the depths of my heart
with their bare skinny bills.
Ah, how clear the reflection of those pelicans is
in the watery mirror.

# 서부호주 퍼스의 백조강변

둥지 틀고 놀다 가고 싶다
한 마리 물새 되어

강 건너 저기 돛폭 접고 정박한
돛대들의 숲에도 가고 싶다

하늘 어디 호수 물결
아무리 눈부셔도

오늘일랑
출렁출렁 푸르른 물결 위로

낮게 낮게
날고 싶다

눈 덮인 산비탈
겨울나목처럼

가슴에 바람 받으며

# Perth: riverside with swans

I want to build a nest and spend some time here.
Becoming a water bird

I want to visit that forest of masts
across the river, moored with sails furled.

No matter how dazzlingly the lake waters
shine somewhere in the sky

today,
I want to go flying

low, low
over the blue rippling waves

feeling the wind blowing on my breast
like a bare winter tree

on some snow-covered mountain slope.

# 정월 대낮

땀구멍에서
땀뿌리가 탄다

포크레인 손갈퀴로 찍어도
찢기지 않을 새파란 하늘

초록앵무새 목 타는 울부짖음에
유카리나무 만신창이로 생살 터지는
서부 호주의 정월 대낮

# January midday

Sweat-roots are burning
in my pores.

A sky so blue it would not tear
if prodded with the prongs of a mechanical digger.

West Australian January midday
as the screeching of parched green parrots
slashes open the raw hides of eucalyptus trees.

# 퍼스의 정오

눈뜨지 말아
눈뜨지 말아

빗발쳐 내리꽂는 직사광선
화살햇살의 폭포수

고막 속 깊은 동굴까지
눈부시게 찢는
우르릉 꽝
순백색의 적막

# Perth, high noon

Don't open your eyes.
Don't open your eyes.

Direct rays raining down
cascades of sunlight-arrows.

Desolation of pure whiteness
ripping into the deep caverns of the ear
dazzling.
Thunder.

# 퍼스의 어느 아침

이곳은 남쪽 나라
노란 열매 익어가는
뒷마당 레몬나무 속에서
비둘기가 알을 품고 있다
하루하루가 창조 닷샛날 같은 이곳
하늘에 깃털구름 쫙 깔려
온 세상을 품은 날
강변에 흩어진 깃털들
어느 둥지에서 날아온 것일까
갈매기 깃털인가
성령의 깃털일까
레몬 향은 바람에 날리고

# One morning in Perth

In this southern land
a pigeon is sitting on her eggs
in a lemon tree in our back garden
with yellow fruits ripening.
Each day here is like the Fifth Day of Creation,
a day when a layer of down was spread in the sky
to keep the world warm.
The down drifting beside the river —
what nest can it have come from?
Is it seagull's down?
Holy Spirit's down?
A scent of lemons drifting in the breeze...

# 하늘반지

여기 탁 - 트인 파아란 하늘이
일망무제 둥글디 둥근 쪽빛
　　　　보석 같았습니다
푸른 향기 가득한 이 사파이어
　　　어느 반지에 단단히 박아
　　　　당신 손가락에 꼬옥
끼워주고 싶었습니다, 밤이 오면


　　　반지 속으로 은하수 흐르고
남국 하늘의 가오리연,
　　　　　긴 꼬리 남십자성
　　　높이 높이 떠올라
　　　천지개벽 이래 최초로
북쪽 밤하늘에 기웃이 돌아
　　　　　당신 어깨 너머로 지도록

# Heavenly ring

The blue sky stretching wide
is like a perfectly round indigo jewel
                    a circle without an end.
I'd like to set that sapphire full of blue perfume
                    firmly in a ring
and slip it on to your finger. When evening comes,


                    as the Milky Way flows into the ring,
the southern sky's stingray kite
                    the long-tailed Southern Cross
                    will fly higher and higher aloft
                    until, at the end of its first journey through
the northern sky since the Creation of the world,
                    it sets aslant over your shoulder there.

# 조개껍질 강물

발그레 물든 아침 강물

배 한 척 지나간다

물결 이랑 고요히 새겨지는 강물

조개껍질 같다

이 오팔빛 조가비 주워서

당신께 보냅니다

화장대 위에 제쳐놓았다가

해 저물면 조갯살 같은 손가락에서

하늘보석 반지 뽑아

거기 담아두세요

# Clam-shell river

On the morning river tinted red

a single boat passes.

The river silently inscribed by a ridge and furrow of waves

is like a clam-shell.

I am sending you this opalescent clam shell

that I picked up.

Set it on your dressing-table

and at sunset drawing the ring with its sky-gems

from your clam-meat-like finger

lay it there.

# 파도바위(Wave Rock)


서부호주 불타는 사막 한복판
바다로부터 4백 킬로 떨어진 곳
파도가 친다. 굳어서
바위로 선 15미터의 물결.
비바람에 깎인 웅장한 파도바위.
출렁임의 절정
무너져내리기 직전, 파도와 파도 사이의
눈부신 고요와 아우성의
영원한 정수리
수평선 떠난 해안의 밀물
땅속 깊이 스며 대륙 한복판에
솟구쳤던 원주민의 춤
아아 어디로 갔는가, 그 출렁대던,
노래의 힘줄들
배암을 움켜쥐고 파도치던 근육,
이렇게도 얌전히 착한 밤의
110미터 길이와 폭 70미터의
침묵으로만 서 있기냐
비바람 속 27억 년
쏟아지는 햇볕 아래
얼마를 더 침묵으로 울어야

# Wave Rock

In the middle of West Australia's scorching desert
400 kilometers from the nearest sea
surf breaks — a wave 15 meters high
frozen, standing, a rock.
Majestic Wave Rock, carved by wind and rain.
Summit of surging
on the very point of breaking, eternal peak
of the dazzling stillness and tumult
between wave and wave,
high tide on a shore that has gone over the horizon,
aborigines' dance that sank deep into the ground
then came leaping up
in the heart of the continent;
ah, what has become
of those surging muscles
of song?
snake-grasping, wave-rolling sinews —
do you stand there so submissive,
the silence of a tender night,
110 meters long, 70 meters wide?
27 billion years in wind and rain
in blazing sunlight —
how much longer must it weep in silence

다시 부서지려는가
넘실대려는가

before it finally breaks
billowing.

# 울루루(Uluru)를 꿈꾸며

나는 아직 울루루에 가지 않았다
그 둥근 잔등 꼭대기에 올라가
양지쪽 건너편 카타주타 봉우리
바라보지 않았다
꿈속에서 아메리칸 인디언 소년들 더불어
들소떼 뒤쫓던 젊은 시절 그대로,
여기 퍼스의 응접실에서 꿈꿀 뿐이다
거대한 조약돌 하나 피에 젖은 모습으로
땅속에서 불쑥 솟아오르듯
꿈틀대며 일어서는 울루루를.
아, 지금 울루루의 음지 쪽
무릎 세운 골짜기 사이
샘물 흘러넘치는 대지의 자궁 근처에서
원주민 하나가
관광객 없던 꿈시간의 울루루를 상상한다

우리는 같은 꿈의 그림을 그리면서
서로를 모른다. 누군가의 피가
땅에서 울부짖는다,
아, 나는 너무 많은 항변을 하지 않았나?

# Dreaming about Uluru

I haven't been to Uluru yet.
I haven't scaled its curving dome
and looked across
at Kata Tjuta rising on the sunny side.
I'm simply dreaming in my Perth living room —
no different from when I was a youngster dreaming of
chasing bison with native American lads —
dreaming about Uluru abruptly rising, twisting
from the ground,
one vast pebble drenched in blood.
Ah, at this very moment,
on the shady side of Uluru
near the womb of the Earth overflowing with spring water
between two rocky knees
one aborigine
is imagining the Uluru of Dreamtime, tourist-free.


We each picture the same image in our dreams,
not knowing one another.
Someone's blood
is crying from the ground.
Oh dear, perhaps I've protested too much?

# 울루루 1

이제 일어나 너를 찾으러 가야 하리
호주 대륙 한복판
달빛에 젖었다 별빛에 마르고
오렌지색에서 도라짓빛으로
눈이 시린 핏빛으로
날씨 따라 색깔 변하며
태양 아래 태산처럼 웅크리고 아직도
펄떡펄떡 피 흘리는

세상에서 제인 큰 바윗덩이
사막 한복판 새벽 제단에
가장 오래된 대륙이
시뻘겋게 꺼내놓은 간덩이
흰머리 독수리들 아직도 허공에
눈빛 사나운 땡볕 세월

백인들이 이름 바꿔
에이어즈 바위(Ayers Rock)라 불러온 울루루
높이 348미터에 둘레가 사십 리
사막의 샘물 지키는 거대한
무지개 구렁이 워남피(Wonampi)가
네 품속에 숨어서 묻고 있다

# Uluru 1

                    I must arise now and go to seek you
          at Australia's heart,
drenched in moonlight, dried in starlight,
              changing color with the weather
                    from orange to purple
           to blinding crimson,
crouching in the sun like the original Great Mountain
                  still pulsating, dripping blood


                  the biggest rock in the world,
          living liver, plucked out crimson
and laid on the early morning altar at the heart of the desert
           by the oldest continent,
           sunshine age of the white-headed eagles
that still eye you fiercely from the sky


          Uluru! The white folk changed your name
and called you Ayers Rock —
          348 meters high, 9 kilometers round
             the great Rainbow Serpent Wanambi
          still hides in your breast,
guarding the desert's springs and asks:

지상 곳곳 죽음보다 새하얀
백인들의 범죄, 용서할 수 있겠느냐
　　　　　폐허에서 날개 펴고 일어설 희망,
버리지 않았느냐


이제 일어나 내 너를 찾으러 가야 하리
호주 대륙 한복판, 아득한 지평선 너머 우뚝 솟아
3억 년 동안 펄떡펄떡 살아 있는 울루루
피흘리는 간덩이

will you be able to forgive the crime of the white folk,
whiter than death here and elsewhere in the world?
Have you not lost that hope that will rise from the ruins
with wings outstretched?

I must arise now and go to seek you
towering aloft at the heart of Australia
beyond the far horizon,
Uluru, palpitating for 300 million years,
fresh, bleeding liver.

# 울루루 2

당신의 소문을 들은 뒤로
나는 당신의 정체를 알기 위해
책들을 뒤지고
사진첩을 모으고 정보의 바다라는
인터넷을 항해해보았지만

뜻밖에도 당신에 관한 글과 사진은
다양하지도 자상하지도 않았습니다
그런 것이 처음에는 불만이었지만
당신 모습이 풍분의 안개 속에
파묻힌 신비인 것이 당연하고
또 다행이라 생각되기도 했습니다

거대한 당신 모습을 그리려는
나의 첫 시도도 다른 글과 사진들처럼
온갖 과장법으로 시작되었습니다
그러나 어떤 과장의 수사도 늘 역부족이었습니다

당신을 만나고 온 오늘은
축소법을 써봅니다
당신은 억센 가시풀 그늘에 웅크린

# Uluru 2


After once hearing rumors about you,
in order to learn what you really were
I ransacked books,
collected photograph albums, went surfing
through the ocean of information on the Internet

but surprisingly the texts and photos about you
were not very varied or detailed.
At first I found that vexing but
then I began to think that it was only natural
and indeed fortunate that your image remained a mystery
wrapped in a fog of rumor.

My first attempts to depict your vastness
like those other texts and photos,
began with all kinds of hyperbole.
But I found every form of exaggeration wanting.

Today, having come to meet you,
I will try using understatement.
You are a scorpion

한 마리 전갈입니다
당신 꼬리에는 사과씨만한 주머니가
달려 있고 그 끝 독침에는
풀씨만한
불씨가 담겨 있을 뿐입니다
그 불씨로
아득한 광야가 삽시간에
치명적인 화염구름에 휩싸이는 때
더러 있었습니다

lurking in the shadow of a tough thornbush.
Attached to your tail is a pouch
the size of an apple seed and in the poisonous sting
at its tip there is nothing but a spark of fire
the size of a grass seed
and there have occasionally been times
when distant plains have been engulfed in a flash
in deadly billows of flame by that spark.

## 울루루 3

세상에서 제일 장엄하고 아름다운 건물 무엇이냐
로마의 베드로 대성전
중국의 자금성
혹은 아, 너무 아름다워 절하고 싶은
타지마할이냐
그 문간에 서면 나는 한 마리 개미

이것들을 호주 대륙 한복판
사막 가운데 우뚝 솟은
원주민들의 자연 성전(聖殿)
시뻘건 통바위 울루루 옆에
옮겨 세우면
모두 개미 한 마리

비행기 타고 발 아래 망망
붉은 모래사막 내려다본다
그림자 길게 드리운
울루루가 한 마리 애벌레처럼 외롭다

# Uluru 3

Which is the most majestic, beautiful building in the world?
St. Peter's Basilica in Rome?
The Forbidden City in Beijing?
Or perhaps the Taj Mahal,
so beautiful one feels inclined to genuflect?
Standing at their gates, I am a mere ant.

If you were to move them
to the heart of Australia
and set them beside the aborigines' natural shrine
the crimson rock Uluru
that soars magnificent in the midst of the desert,
they would each be a mere ant.

From the plane I look down
at the red sand stretching far, without end.
Uluru with its long-stretching shadow
looks lonely as a baby larva.

# 울루루 4

통바위산 울루루 산정에는 여기 저기
마른 웅덩이 패어 있어
방패새우들이 먼지와 모래 속에 알들로 섞여
잠시 잠들었다가 폭우라도 쏟아져 웅덩이에
물 고이면 황망히 알에서 깨어나
새끼손톱만큼 서둘러 자라면서 알을 깐다. 햇볕 쏟아져
물기 지글지글 증발하면 한 시간짜리 일생도
순식간에 벼랑이다
울루루 서북쪽 골짝에는 사막가뭄에도 일 년 열두 달
마르지 않는 샘물 있고 서늘한 동굴도 있는데,
이상한 일이다, 도마뱀도 캥거루도 원주민도
벌들도 새들도 불볕더위 석 달 열흘 계속되는
가장 어려운 때 잠시 찾아와
목을 축이고는 곧 떠난다
그 누구도 이 오아시스에
영주권 시민권 원치 않는다
심한 비바람 모진 추위 견디기 어려우면
바위굴에 며칠 몸 의탁하다가 어디론가 사라진다
누군가 여기 정착하여 울타리 치고 독차지했으면
사막의 뭇 생명 옛날에 옛날에 모두 사라졌으리

# Uluru 4

At the summit of Uluru's huge monolith
dry pools lie hollowed out here and there where
shield-shrimps mingle as eggs with dust and sand
then after sleeping a while, if a shower falls and
water gathers in the pools, they
hurriedly awake, grow to the size of baby fingertips,
lay eggs. Sunlight pours down
the water evaporates and one hour's worth of life
is done in a flash.
In a valley to the northwest of Uluru there is a cool cave
with a spring that never dries up even in desert drought;
strange to say, lizards and kangaroos, aborigines and bees
and birds, only at the harshest time when blazing heat
continues unceasing for three months and ten days,
make a brief visit, quench their thirst,
then quickly move away.
None of them desires permanent residence or citizenship
in that oasis.
When a fierce gale or bitter cold are hard to bear they
take shelter in the cave for a few days, then vanish again.
If someone were to settle here, build a wall, take possession,
every kind of desert life would have vanished long, long ago.

# 울루루 5

이집트에 피라미드가 있다면
호주에는 울루루가 있다
피라미드가 역사라면
울루루는 꿈이다
기하학에 기댄 역사의 영원은 매일이 사막이고
자연의 사막은 매일 꿈을 꾼다
물안개 뿜어 무지개 만들며
헤엄쳐 이동하는 고래떼를

# Uluru 5

While Egypt has its pyramids
Australia has Uluru.
While pyramids can be considered history
Uluru is dream.
The permanence of history backed up by geometry
is daily desert; the natural desert daily dreams.
Herds of whales swim on their way
spouting mist and making rainbows.

# 울루루 6


혀푸른도마뱀의 갈라진 혀보다 더 새파란
이 절망은 무엇인가
구름 한 점 없는 하늘 여섯 달
붉은 모래알보다 더 붉은
이 사막의 울음은 무엇인가
너 시뻘건 울음덩이 울루루
붉디붉은 알몸의 바위
해지고 달 뜨니 오늘밤은
잘 삶은 간덩이처럼 퍽퍽할 것 같구나

# Uluru  6

What is this despair,
bluer than a blue-tongued lizard's forked tongue?
What are this desert's tears,
redder than grains of red sand
under a sky quite cloudless six months of the year?
You, Uluru, crimson mass of tears,
naked bright red rock,
tonight, when the sun sets and the moon rises,
you will be dry and powdery like well-cooked liver.

# 봄처녀

그녀의 온몸에서
색색의 나비들이 날아오른다
손끝을 방금 떠난 나비
발가락에서 날갯짓하는 나비
젖꼭지에서 더듬이를 말고 있는 나비
땀구멍에서 겨드랑이에서
그리고 사타구니에서
연둣빛 날개 파르르 떨며
머리카락 사이로 기어나오는 나비
3월이 겨울잠에서
막 깨어나는 중이다
냇물, 토끼풀, 호박벌의 이름으로
나무관세음보살

# Springtime maiden

From every part of the girl's body
multicolored butterflies come flying up.
The butterfly that has just left her finger
the butterfly flapping its wings on a toe
the butterfly unrolling its antennae on a nipple
the butterflies emerging from her pores
her armpits, her groin
from between the hairs of her head
fluttering pale yellow wings.
March is waking
from its winter sleep.
In the name of the streams, the clover, the bumble bee,
thanks be to you, merciful Avalokitesvara.

# 바람 부는 날

옷 찢어질 듯 바람 거센 날
갈매기들이 일제히 바람 부는 쪽을 향하여
바람을 바라보며 앉아 있다

나는 바람 등지고 나무에 기대어
세찬 바람 피하지 않는
고매한 관풍(觀楓)의 정신을 사유하는데

엄숙 심각하게 폼잡을 것 하나도 없다
억센 바람 어째서 온몸으로 껴안는지
자 한번 보라는 듯
난해한 까닭 같은 거
하나도 없다는 듯

머리칼 멋지게 휘날리며
바람과 이마받이하던 갈매기 한 마리가
과자 부스러기 찍어먹으려 잠깐
바람을 등지는 순간

# A windy day

On a day with a wind strong enough to rip off your clothes
all the seagulls without exception are perched facing
the direction the wind's blowing from, looking into the wind.

As I shelter from the wind behind a tree,
I meditate on their noble attitude of mind
as they refuse to avoid the gale.

There's nothing serious to put on airs about.
As if to invite me to look and see
why it so wholeheartedly embraces the fierce wind, or
as if to say there's no kind of abstruse reason for it at all,

one seagull that had been butting at the wind
with the plumes on its head streaming smartly
turned its back briefly
to grab a scrap of biscuit

겉털 속털 날개깃털 홀러덩
뒤집혀
똥구멍 밑구멍까지 죄다
드러나는 것이었다

and in a flash the feathers on sides, breast and wings
turned inside out,
exposing
the asshole under its tail, and all.

# 역사와 시인

역사는 음험한 포주
우리들 하나하나를
화냥년으로 팔아넘긴다

시인은 우물가에서 화냥년 만나
물 한 바가지 청해
그녀의 끝끝내 숫처녀 시절
남실남실
넘치는 샘물

시원스레 쭉 들이켜는 사람이다

# History and the poet

History's a sinister pimp
selling off each of us
as a whore.

A poet is whoever meets a whore by a well
requests a scoopful of water,
the water overflowing
dancing
of her living, virgin days

and freely drinks.

# 『한국문학 영역총서』를 펴내며

한국문학을 본격적으로 번역하여 해외에 소개하는 일이 필요함을 우리는 오래 전부터 절실히 느껴 왔다. 그러나 좋은 번역을 만나기는 좋은 창작품을 만나는 것 못지 않게 어렵다. 운이 좋아서 좋은 번역이 있을 경우에는 또한 출판의 기회를 얻기가 쉽지 않다. 서구의 유수한 출판사들은 시장성을 앞세워 지명도가 높지 않은 한국의 문학작품을 출판하기를 꺼린다. 한국문학의 지명도가 높아지려면 먼저 훌륭하게 번역된 작품들이 세계적인 명성이 있는 출판사에서 출판이 되어 널리 보급이 되어야 하는데, 설혹 훌륭한 번역이 있다 하더라도 이 작품들이 해외에서 출판될 기회가 극히 제한되어 있어서, 지명도를 높일 길이 막막해지는 악순환을 거듭하는 것이 현실이다. 이런 현실을 타개하는 길은 좋은 작품을 제대로 번역하여 우리 손으로 쾌답게 출판하여 세계의 독자들에게 내놓는 데서 찾을 수밖에 없다. 이런 일을 하기 위해 도서출판 답게에서 "한국문학 영역총서"를 세상에 내놓는다.

「답게」영역총서는 한영 대역판으로 출판되며, 이 총서는 광범위한 독자층을 위하여 만들어진 것이다. 무엇보다도 이 총서를 통해 해외의 많은 문학 독자들이 한국문학을 알게 되기를 희망한다. 이 총서는 또한 국내외에서 한국학을 공부하거나 영어로 번역된 한국 작품을 필요로 하는 영어 사용권의 모든 사람들과 한국문학의 전문적인 번역자들을 위한 것이기도 하다. 전문 번역인들은 동료 번역자들의 작업을 자신들의 것과 비교함으로써 보다 나은 새로운 번역 방법을 모색할 수 있을 것이다. 고급한 영어를 배우기를 원하는 한국의 독자들도 대역판으로 출간되는 이 총서를 읽음으로써, 언어가 어떻게 문학적으로 신비롭게 또 절묘하게 쓰이는지를 깨닫는 등 많은 것을 얻을 수 있을 것이다.

아무리 말쑥하게 잘 만들어진 책이라도 그 내용이 신통치 않으면 결코 책다운 책일 수 없다는 자명한 이유에서,「답게」영역총서는 좋은 작품을 골라 최선의 질로 번역한 책만을 출판할 것이다. 또한 새로운 번역자의 발굴과 격려가 이 총서 발간의 목적 가운데 하나이다. 답게 출판사가 발행하는 이 총서가 한국문학의 번역의 중요성을 다시 한 번 일깨우고, 문학 작품의 번역이라는 불가능한 꿈을 가능하게 하려는 번역자들의 노력에 보탬이 되기를 바란다. 이런 시도가 여러 가지로 유용하고 또 도전적인 것이 될 때, 더 나아가서는 잘 번역된 한국 작품의 전세계적인 출판 작업이 이루어지는 단초를 마련할 수 있을 때, 이 선구적인 계획은 진정으로 성공적인 것이 될 것이다.

김 영 무 (서울대 영문과 교수)

# Series Editor's Afterword

Extensive translation of Korean literature for the foreign readers has for many years been felt a pressing need. But to fall upon a good translation is much harder than to discern a good original work. If we are fortunate enough to secure a good translation, it is often very difficult to get it published abroad.

The major publishers of the western world are not yet prepared to run the risk of publishing works of relatively unknown Korean literature. Yet if Korean literature is to achieve worldwide fame, it first of all needs to be well translated, and then put into circulation throughout the world by those very publishers which are so reluctant to publish even good translations of Korean literature. It is a vicious circle : no publication without fame but no fame without publication. To save the situation, we should perhaps try to make available to readers abroad choice translations we ourselves have published in editions of high quality. The DapGae English Translations of Korean Literature series has been launched with this aim.

Each volume of the DapGae series will be a bilingual edition. We expect a wide-ranging audience for the series. It is our primary hope that it will help introduce many foreign readers to the world of Korean literature. The series is especially intended to serve English-speaking students enrolled in Korean studies programs and all who need translations of Korean literature, as well as those who may wish to compare their own translations with the translations of fellow translators in order to find new and better ways of translating. Korean readers studying advanced English can also benefit from reading these bilingual editions : the experience may help them to recognize the mystery of true mastery of the literary use of language.

However well designed a book may be, it cannot properly serve its purpose if the contents are mediocre. For that reason, the DapGae series will strive to introduce to the readers of the world the best translations of the finest works of Korean literature. One of the objectives of the series is to find and encourage new talents in English translation. We hope that the DapGae English Translations of Korean Literature series will serve in some small way to refocus attention upon the importance of translating Korean literature into good English and to make possible the impossible dream of literary translation. This pioneering project will be a true success not only if it proves useful and challenging but also if it paves the way for the publication of fine translations of Korean literature on a worldwide scale.

Young-Moo Kim
Department of English
Seoul National University

# 역자 소개

● 안토니 수사

프랑스 초교파 수도원 테제 공동체의 수사. 1942년 영국에서 태어나 1980년부터 한국에서 거주하였다. 서강대학교 교수로 영문학을 가르치면서 김영무와 함께 고은의 <나의 파도 소리>와 선시 <뭐냐>, 천상병의 <귀천>, 신경림의 <농무>, 김수영, 신경림, 이시영 시선집을 영어로 옮겼다.

● 이종숙

서울대학교 영어영문학과 교수. *Ben Jonson's Poesis: A Literary Dialectic of Ideal and History* (Charlottesville, VA.: University of Virginia Press, 1989)의 저자로, 셰익스피어와 르네상스 영문학에 대한 논문을 다수 발표했으며, 칠레의 저항시인 아리엘 도르프만의 시집 <싼띠아고에서의 마지막 왈츠>를 번역한 바 있다.

# The Translators

**Brother Anthony** of Taizé, is a member of the Community of Taizé (France). Born in Britain in 1942, he has lived in Korea since 1980. He is a professor in the English department of Sogang University, Seoul. Kim Young-Moo and Brother Anthony together translated *The Sound of my Waves* and *Beyond Self* by Ko Un, *Back to Heaven* by Ch'ŏn Sang-Pyŏng, *Variations* by Kim Su-Yŏng, Shin Kyŏng-Nim, and Lee Si-Yŏng, and *Farmers' Dance* by Shin Kyŏng-Nim.

**Jongsook Lee**, Professor of English at Seoul National University, Seoul, Korea, has written numerous articles on Shakespeare and the English Renaissance, and is the author of *Ben Jonson's Poesis: A Literary Dialectic of Ideal and History* (Charlottesville, VA.: University of Virginia Press, 1989). Professor Lee is the Korean translator of Ariel Dorfman's book of poetry, *Last Waltz in Santiago*.

저자와
협의하여
인지 생략

# 가상현실

지은이 | 김영무
옮긴이 | 안선재(안토니 수사) · 이종숙
펴낸이 | 一庚 張少任
펴낸곳 | 답게 (나답게 우리답게 책답게)

초판 발행 | 2005년 6월 23일
초판 2쇄 | 2005년 8월 18일

등 록 | 1990년 2월 28일, 제 21-140호
주 소 | 137-834 서울시 서초구 방배4동 829-22호 원빌딩 201호
전 화 | 02)532-4867(대표) 02)591-8267(편집기획팀)
        02)596-0464, 02)537-0464(영업관리팀)
팩 스 | 02)594-0464
홈페이지 | www.dapgae.co.kr
e-mail | dapgae@chollian.net, dapgae@korea.com

ISBN 89-7574-184-2 02810

✱ 책값은 뒤표지에 있습니다.
✱ 잘못 만들어진 책은 구입하신 서점에서 교환해 드립니다.